This is a first edition published in 2020 by Flying Eye Books,
an imprint of Nobrow Ltd. 27 Westgate Street, London E8 3RL.

Written by Stephen Davies and illustrated by Sapo Lendario,
based on the characters and storylines
created by Luke Pearson and Silvergate Media company.

HILDA™ © 2020 Hilda Productions Limited,
a Silvergate Media company

1 3 5 7 9 10 8 6 4 2

Published in the US by Nobrow (US) Inc.

Printed in Great Britain on FSC® certified paper.

MIX
Paper from
responsible sources
FSC® C020471

ISBN: 978-1-912497-58-4

Order from www.flyingeyebooks.com

Based on the Hildafolk series of graphic novels by Luke Pearson

HILDA
AND THE
WHITE WOFF

Written by Stephen Davies   Illustrated by Sapo Lendário

FLYING EYE BOOKS

London | New York

CONTENTS

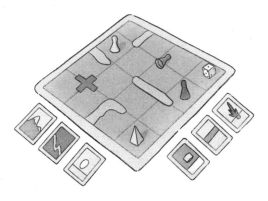

Rain poured. A deer fox snored. A house spirit gazed at a Dungeon Crops board. In the corner of the living room, a little girl with blue hair was babbling excitedly into a telephone.

"Frida, that sounds amazing... yes, of course I want to come with you... wouldn't miss it for the world!"

Hilda went into the kitchen, where Mom was busy spooning hot-chocolate powder into mugs.

"Sorry, Mom," said Hilda. "Slight change of plan. I need to go and meet Frida."

Mom frowned. "I thought we were going to play our new board game."

"Sorry," said Hilda again. "I do want to play Dungeon Crops soon, but Frida says she needs help with some homework she's got."

Mom poured hot milk into each of the three mugs and stirred it briskly. "Frida? Needs your help? With homework?"

"Don't sound so surprised!" laughed Hilda, pouring hot chocolate into a Thermos and slipping it into her adventuring satchel. She ran into the hall and grabbed her scarf and beret from a peg. "Frida says I can sleep over if I want to. Is that all right, Mom? Please say yes!" Hilda scooped up Twig and squashed him against the side of her face, big-eyed and pouting.

"All right," said Mom, "but I want you back here in time for lunch tomorrow, is that clear?"

"Hooray!" Hilda punched the air and twirled on her toes. "Thanks, Mom, you're the best! Come on, Twig! Bye, Tontu! Sorry about Dungeon Crops. We'll play tomorrow. Bye!"

With Twig at her heels, Hilda dashed out of the apartment, down three flights of stairs, and out into the fresh air. She jumped on her bike and rode off, pedalling hard.

The rain eased off a little as Hilda coasted through the maze of apartment blocks and out onto Fredrik Street. As soon as she was on the main road, she leaned low over the handlebars and picked up speed. Twig galloped behind, ears flapping in the wind.

As she sped through the city gate and north toward the wilderness, Hilda did feel a pang of conscience for the half-truths she had told Mom. It was true that Frida had asked for help with homework, but it was witching homework, not schoolwork. And it was true that they were planning a sleepover—just not at Frida's house.

Frida and David were already waiting for her on the edge of the Great Forest. Their mission, Frida explained, was to collect dust from the ruins of Fort Ahlberg. Ancient castle dust was an essential ingredient for the invisibility spell that she was trying to learn.

The three friends hid their bikes inside giant roffleworts and set off westward into the trees. Frida and David carried huge camping backpacks and Hilda wore her smaller adventuring satchel. They agreed to swap when one of them got tired.

David had camped at Camp Sparrow several times, but this was his first time camping outside the city walls.

"What if we meet a troll after sundown?" he kept asking.

"Relax," said Hilda. "We'll have the castle dust by then so Frida can just make us all invisible."

"Exactly," said Frida, but she sounded more certain than she looked.

They came to a narrow river where canary grass waved in the breeze and weeping willows stooped to brush the babbling water. Hilda took a long run up, jumped through the air and landed in a giggling heap on the far side of the river. Frida followed and then Twig, soaring gracefully like a champion showjumper.

"Your turn, David!" they called.

David lowered his head and pawed the ground like a bull preparing to charge, but then he straightened up again. "Sorry," he said. "I don't dare risk it."

No amount of encouragement could persuade David to attempt the jump. In the end, they had to leap back across the river and search for another place to cross.

Half a mile further downstream, a pine tree had fallen across the river, creating a natural bridge.

"It's like a balance beam!" cried Frida, prancing across the tree trunk with her arms out to her sides.

"You may as well come back now," muttered David. "There's no way I'm walking across that thing."

Hilda took David's heavy backpack and gave him her light adventuring satchel, but still he refused to cross the pine tree bridge. "I'm slowing you down," he sighed. "I should just go home and let you two carry on without me."

"Don't be silly," said Hilda. "I'm sure we can find an easier crossing point."

The walk continued like this all afternoon. David refused to use the stepping stones because they looked too slippery. He refused to take a shortcut through a glade of twisted yew trees because he imagined there might be a troll rock in the middle. Later, as the sun sank low in the west and shadows lengthened, his face turned pale and he jumped at every sound. Hilda tried to cheer him up by making up a river-crossing puzzle involving a troll, a goat, and a sack of grain, but this just scared him even more.

It was dark by the time they arrived at Fort Ahlberg. They shrugged off their backpacks and stood in silence, gazing in awe at the ancient, jagged ramparts and half-ruined walls.

While Frida collected dust, Hilda climbed the castle walls. The great, gray stones were pitted and scarred, offering plenty of natural hand and footholds. Hilda climbed quickly, except for one awkward overhang where she had to take her feet off the wall and haul herself up by her fingertips.

When she reached the summit of the ruined turret, she stood up and leaned into the wind, as high and free as a migrating woff. In front of her, the dense canopy of iron pine, birch, and bludbok trees stretched away toward the snow-capped mountains of the north, where a hundred troll fires crackled and popped.

"Be careful!" yelled David down below.

"I will!" Hilda called back.

As her eyes adjusted to the darkness, she noticed a pyramid of rectangular boulders poking up through the canopy about five miles away.

"Hey, guys!" she exclaimed. "You'll never guess what I've spotted. It's the Screaming Stones!"

2

Hilda slithered down the castle walls and landed in a pile of leaves. Frida and David ran and helped her up.

"I know I'm going to regret asking this question," said David, "but what are the Screaming Stones?"

"Just what they sound like," said Hilda. "Emil Gammelplassen mentions them in his new book, *Swamps and Their Unfriendly Occupants*. He heard them himself one night, when he was camping in the forest. They were shrieking and wailing and screeching like harpies, but by the time he reached them the following morning, they were silent."

"I see," said David, his face pale in the moonlight. "Can we please go home now?"

"No David," said Frida. "We'll camp here and go home in the morning."

The children pitched their tent in a circle of moonlight inside the castle walls and built a fire nearby. They pronged veggie sausages on sticks and cooked them over the flames.

"What if the trolls see our fire?" quavered David.

"They'll think it's a troll fire," said Frida. "There

are so many troll fires around Trolberg these days, one more won't make a difference."

Ten minutes later, they were all cozy inside the tent with a splendid feast laid out between them: a dozen piping-hot sausages, two crusty baguettes, a packet of ginger cookies, Hilda's flask of hot chocolate, and a bowl of rowanberries from a nearby bush. Their long hike had made them hungry, and they tucked gratefully into their meal.

Frida watched Hilda blow on a sausage to cool it down for Twig. "You two are so cute," she said. "How did you first meet?"

"It's kind of a long story."

"Perfect," said Frida. "I like long stories."

Hilda bit into a ginger cookie. "It was five years ago," she said, speaking with her mouth full, "and I was out in the wilderness, walking with my mom. I heard a strange noise coming from a pile of fallen rocks at the bottom of a slope, so I scrambled down the bank to investigate, and there in front of me was this tiny little creature with a fluffy tail and twig-like antlers. His paw was trapped between the rocks, poor thing, so I pried them apart to set him free."

"Wonderful," said Frida. "And you've been together ever since?"

"No," said Hilda. "Twig ran off into the bushes and I didn't see him again until two years later, which was the day I fell off a cliff."

"You fell off a cliff?" David gasped. "Which cliff?"

"The one on the north bank of the fjord, where the razorbeak eagles nest. And before you ask, I didn't just fall off a cliff for no reason. I was distracted by something I saw."

"What?"

"I'm not even sure how to describe it. It was this weird, glowing path slanting up into the sky on the opposite side of the fjord. A flock of little creatures was parading weightlessly upward along the path of light."

"What kind of creatures?"

"Deer foxes. But at the time I was too far away to see what they were, so I did what anybody would have done. I stepped forward to get a better view."

"And fell off the cliff," said David.

"Yes." Hilda winced at the memory. "I fell about

ten yards and landed on a narrow ledge half-way down the cliff face. I'll never forget lying there looking down at the foaming waves below, and the salt lions staring up at me, licking their lips."

David gulped. "I don't feel very well," he said. "Maybe you could tell us the rest another time."

"Relax, David," said Frida, taking another ginger biscuit. "This is the best story ever. What did you do then, Hilda?"

"I started screaming for help, of course. Mom was up at the top of the cliff, but she couldn't find a way down to me. And then I noticed a nest of baby eagles beside me on the ledge. Tiny little critters with big eyes and fuzzy heads."

"Cute," said Frida.

"Yes. But their mother was less cute."

"Oh, no!"

"Oh, yes." Hilda lowered her voice to a whisper and angled her flashlight upward so that her chin and cheekbones were illuminated by a spooky light. "There was an ear-piercing shriek and before I knew what was happening, the mother eagle swooped out of the sky and pounced on me, flapping, pecking, and scrabbling. She forced me off the ledge until my feet were dangling in mid-air and I was holding on with just my fingertips, knowing that any second now I was going to—"

"Stop!" cried David. "I don't want to hear any more!" He crawled across the tent on all fours, unzipped the opening and ran into the night. Cold wind blew inside the tent, making Hilda and Frida gasp and shiver.

Frida reached over to zip up the entrance. "What then?"

"I looked up," said Hilda, "and I saw something so strange, I thought I must be imagining it. A pure, white creature floating down from the sky, surrounded by twinkling lights."

"Twig!" cried Frida.

"That's right," said Hilda. "He was a bit bigger than before, and his antlers were sharper, but I recognized him straight away."

"I didn't know deer foxes could fly!"

"They can't. But it turns out that every spring there is a mysterious event called the Great Deer Fox Migration. There's a whole book about it at the library. All of the deer foxes in the northern counties gather together into one enormous flock and up they go, on this magical luminous escalator."

Frida clasped her hands together, hanging on Hilda's every word.

"Anyway, Twig grabbed me by the collar of my sweater and somehow managed to haul me back up onto the ledge. And when the eagle started attacking again, Twig put his head down and fended it off with his antlers. He led me all the way along the ledge and found a safe path back up to the top of the cliff."

"Wow."

Hilda reached out and scratched Twig behind his ears. "You missed your opportunity to migrate,

didn't you boy? You let your friends carry on without you, and you came and saved my life."

Twig stretched forward and nuzzled Hilda with his shiny black nose. Frida unzipped the entrance to the tent and poked her head out.

"David!" she called. "The story's finished. You can come back now!"

Silence.

"I wonder where he's gone," said Frida.

"Twig will find him," said Hilda. "Won't you, boy?"

Twig arched his back, blinked twice, and padded out into the night.

3

David hurried through the woods, his heart still pounding. Heights, birds of prey, and salt lions were three of his greatest fears, so Hilda's story had really given him goosebumps. Not until he was far away from the tent did he remember that his three other greatest fears were darkness, spooky forests, and being all alone.

"Why do I have to be such a scaredy-cat?" he said out loud. He tutted angrily and kicked a patch of moss, which promptly uprooted itself and fled on spindly legs. David yelped in horror.

He was really nervous now. He stopped dead in his tracks, listening to the eerie scratchings and rustlings of the forest. Then he heard a growl close by and felt something brush against his ankle.

David leaped backward, lost his footing, and fell head first down a steep slope. It's only Twig, he reassured himself on the way down, and that was his last thought before passing out.

When David came to, he was propped up against the wall of a cave and a man in chain mail was bandaging his head. David jerked back in shock.

"Fear not," said the man. "I'm here to help. I found you and your pet at the bottom of the hill."

David looked around. Flaming torches cast flickering shadows across the cave walls, and the floor was littered with pottery and animal bones. In the center, meat was roasting over a fire and gathered around it sat a horde of men who looked like the Vikings in David's picture books at home. They were drinking from clay goblets and sharpening fearsome-looking weapons.

"You'll have a lump on your head," said the

man, "but your injuries are nothing compared to Olaf over there." He gestured airily toward a one-armed, one-eyed man in a horned helmet.

David stared. "You're... you're... you're Vikings," he stammered.

"Indeed we are," chuckled the man. "I am Torgund, Warrior of Thunder. And you are...?"

"David."

What would Hilda do in this situation? David wondered. Ask the Vikings all about themselves, probably, and then join them on some wild adventure. But Hilda he was not.

"Thanks for patching me up," said David, standing up unsteadily. "I should be going now. My friends will be worried."

Torgund frowned. "You're not leaving already, are you? You'll miss your chance to show bravery in battle!"

"Exactly." David looked round wildly for an exit to the cave. "You see, the thing about bravery is, I don't have any."

"Aha!" Torgund slapped a big hand on David's shoulder. "If it's bravery you need, you're in luck.

We came to this valley seeking the Medallion of Sigurd. They say that all who touch it will be fearless for the rest of their days."

David stared at the Viking's furrowed brow and the torchlight dancing in his eyes. "You're saying I could be fearless?"

"That is precisely what I'm saying," said Torgund, his voice low and serious. "Only one thing stands in our way, and that's the Knudsen clan. Those brigands stole the medallion before we could claim it, so we're going to slay every last one of them!"

"Oh." David stared at the Viking.
"That sounds... fair."

"Do you know how to use a sword?"

"No."

"Battle ax?"

"No."

"Damage-hammer?" Torgund held up a strange, spiky club.

"Certainly not," said David.

Torgund's eyes sparkled. "Then you shall be our messenger on the battlefield! Come, David, eat with us, and then we shall sally forth together to paint the valley red with Knudsen blood."

The mention of blood and the sight of one-eyed, one-armed Olaf devouring a rack of ribs made David completely lose his appetite. He offered his portion of meat to Twig, who turned up his nose. After the meal, the Vikings sang a hearty battle song, banging their shields with their swords and axes. Twig's hackles rose along his back, and he whimpered quietly.

"I'm scared, too, boy," David whispered, "but that's why I've got to touch the medallion. I'm tired of holding Hilda and Frida back."

The Vikings' battle song rose to a crescendo and ended with a barbaric roar. In a frenzy of excitement, they raised their weapons and rushed out of the cave. Through the forest the Vikings strode, and David tagged along. Bludbok leaves and birch twigs rustled and crunched under their boots, and the moon cast dabs of silvery light across their painted shields.

All of a sudden, Torgund stopped and raised a hand for silence. The warriors tensed, peering into the darkness ahead of them, sniffing the cold night air for clues.

The sound of voices reached David's ears. They sounded happy, triumphant even, and one in particular stood out among the chatter. "Gaze upon it, men! The perfect prize that drives out fear!"

"Knudsen," Torgund mouthed, and he gestured for his men to move forward silently. In the clearing ahead of them, a battalion of soldiers was gathered round their chief. Moonlight glinted off a large, round amulet in the chief's hand.

"The Medallion of Sigurd," murmured David. "One touch, and I'll be brave for the rest of my life. Just think of that! I'll swim Bjorg Fjord, freeclimb the Glittercliffs, wrestle trolls, ride woffs, and cross rickety bridges over yawning chasms. I'll never hold my friends back again."

Torgund's men fanned out around the edge of the clearing.

As for Knudsen, he had not yet spotted the danger. "When we take this medallion home,' he said, "all of our countrymen will touch it, and all of them will be instantly freed from fear!"

"You'll do no such thing!" declared Torgund.

Knudsen looked up and saw that he and his men were surrounded. He drew a mighty sword from his scabbard and let out a deafening roar.

"CHARGE!!!"

A thousand startled birds woke from their sleep and billowed up into the night sky. The Knudsen clan thundered forward, swords and damage-hammers at the ready.

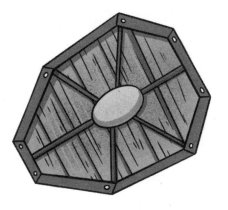

The Knudsens charged toward their foes, their chain mail sparkling purple and gold. But Torgund, Warrior of Thunder, stayed low behind his shield.

"Fight smart, men," urged Torgund. "They have the medallion, but we have our skill and our good sense. Sit tight and wait for my command."

The Knudsens were just ten yards away.

"Hold the line!" cried Torgund.

Five yards.

"Hold fast!" cried Torgund.

Two yards.

"Not yet!" cried Torgund.

BOOM!

Torgund's men rocked back on their heels as Knudsen swords assailed their shields. They winced at the clash of steel on steel but still they held the line.

"Now!" cried the Warrior of Thunder, and with the speed of a striking viper, he emerged from behind his shield and swung his damage-hammer at the warrior in front of him. The hammer fizzed and sparkled with magical energy, and the enemy's head flew clean off his shoulders.

"Gross!" squealed David, horrified.

Torgund's clansmen had all leaped out at the exact same moment, startling their attackers with the suddenness and ferocity of their counterattack. Swords chopped. Axes lopped. Deadly damage-hammers bopped. Everyone's weapons glowed and sparkled as if blessed by some mystical force.

From the middle of the melee, Torgund's voice boomed loud and clear. "Messenger boy, I summon you!"

"Oh, cruddlesticks!" muttered David.

David headed toward Torgund, doing his best to avoid the most violent skirmishes. He ran like a cat on hot bricks, jumping and flinching all the way. "Ai!" he cried, tripping over someone's leg. "Oo!" he squealed as a sword whistled over his head. "Ee!" he yelped, as he dodged an enormous ball made up of wrestling Vikings.

When David arrived at Torgund's side, he was rewarded with a grizzled smile. "Good lad!" said Torgund. "Go and tell Bjarnsen to bring up the right flank!"

David set off running again. "Bjarnsen?" he called. "Message for Bjarnsen!"

"Over there," grunted a nearby soldier, jerking his thumb toward the east side of the clearing. A barrel-chested warrior stood in the moonlight, swinging a mighty ax around his head, felling countless foes with every swing.

David crouched low and hurried across the clearing, trying to make himself as small and inconspicuous as possible. "Hey Bjarnsen," he hissed when he got close. "Torgund says to bring up the right flank."

"I just did," said Bjarnsen, as another whirl of his ax sent three more of Knudsen's men flying.

"Oh," said David. "Good job."

Bjarnsen held out the battle ax toward David. "Give this to Elof," he said.

David took the ax in both hands, staggered a few paces and fell down in the mud. He hauled himself to his feet, picked up the ax again, dropped it again, picked it up again, dropped it again, picked it up, dropped it, picked it up, dropped it, picked it up, dragged it a few paces through the mud, and finally dropped it again.

"Elof!" he yelled. "Ax for Elof?"

There was no response, except for the clash of metal on metal, and lots of enthusiastic shrieking.

Light fell on Hilda's eyelids. She frowned, sat up and rubbed her eyes.

"Hilda, is that you?" came a voice from the sleeping bag beside her. The bag was zipped up tight and a few locks of hair poked out the top.

"I had the most peculiar dream," said Hilda. "We were in a maths lesson at school and Miss Hallgrim was telling us about right-angled triangles when suddenly Erik Ahlberg burst into the classroom and started screaming and yelling."

Frida sat bolt upright and opened up her sleeping bag. "There was screaming in my dream, too," she said.

The same thought struck both girls at precisely the same moment. The Screaming Stones.

"The screaming wasn't just in our dreams, it was actually happening!" said Hilda. "I can't believe we didn't wake up. We could have gone and sketched—"

"Wait!" Frida interrupted sharply. "Where's David?"

Hilda looked over at David's sleeping bag, which had clearly not been slept in. She remembered him leaving last night, and Twig going out to search for him, and she and Frida lying down to wait for them, and the pleasant feeling of warmth and fullness, and the waves of tiredness spreading through her body. It had been such a long, exhausting day.

"We fell asleep!" cried Hilda, horrified. "Poor David's been out all night. And Twig! Where on earth are they?"

"Knock, knock! Rise and shine!"

Hilda and Frida looked at each other. The voice sounded like David's, but there was something different about it—it was louder and more confident than usual.

David unzipped the entrance and peered in. He did not look like someone who had passed a sleepless night. On the contrary, he looked fresh-

faced and full of energy.

"Come on, you layabouts!" he shouted. "Seize the day by the horns! We'd better get a move on if we want to get to those Screaming Stones!"

"Where did you go last night?" asked Hilda. "We were worried about you."

"Oh, here and there," said David, cramming his sleeping bag back into his backpack. "Generally living my best life. Why sleep the day away when you can spend it performing marvellous feats of bravery?"

"It wasn't the day," muttered Hilda, climbing out of her sleeping bag. "It was the night."

David threw a rowanberry into the air and caught it in his mouth. Then he hoisted his backpack onto one shoulder and disappeared outside.

"What a transformation!" smiled Frida. "Why's he acting so strange?"

"I've got no idea," whispered Hilda. "But we'd better get a move on. He's already packing up the tent."

The tent began to sag in the middle, then one

side collapsed completely. Hilda and Frida shoved their sleeping bags into a backpack and wriggled out just in time to avoid being engulfed.

With a sudden burst of energy, David crammed the entire tent into his backpack, then raised a juice box into the air for a toast. "To your good health!" he exclaimed. "And to the success of our great journey!"

They set off northward in the direction of the Screaming Stones. All around them, the forest was waking up. A linnet twittered in the treetops. A squirrel bounded overhead. A pair of

woodchucks foraged on the ground.

"Oh, how much wood would a woodchuck chuck, if a woodchuck could chuck wood?" sang David, striding along in the lead. "Stay out of my way, woodchucks, or I'll chuck you into the middle of next week!"

"David!" said Frida. "There's a bug on your head."

David darted off the path and banged his forehead nine times against a tree trunk. "Got him!" he cried, "and I'll do the same to any other pest that lands upon my noble pate."

They came to a river and walked alongside it, David thrashing at reeds with a stick.

"Ha! Yah! No foolish grass will stand in my way! Ha! Yah! The Screaming Stones await!"

Hilda heard the sound of a waterfall up ahead. Their pathway petered out and the river cascaded over the edge of a cliff, thundering down into the plunge pool below.

"We need to be really careful here," said Frida, consulting the Sparrow Scout Manual. "According to this, we need to affix a safety tether and rappel gently down the side of the—"

"Wooo-hooo!" shrieked David, and before they could stop him, he sprinted past them and took a gigantic leap off the edge of the waterfall. "Geronimooooo!" he cried as he disappeared into the misty spray below. "Woweee," he yelled as he resurfaced, laughing. "I feel incredible!"

Hilda and Frida exchanged an incredulous look as David swam to the safety of the bank. "Who are you?" Hilda yelled, "and what have you done with David?"

5

The walk continued in this way, with David's antics ranging from brave to irresponsible to completely reckless. The scariest moment of all was when they spotted a brown bear rubbing its back on the bark of a nearby tree trunk. Twig and the girls tiptoed past, careful not to attract the bear's attention, but David had other ideas.

"HEY, YOU FUZZY BOZO!" he yelled at the top of his voice. "GET OUT OF OUR WAY!"

The bear straightened up and looked at David. It reared up on its hind legs and let out a menacing growl. Twig's hackles rose and his tail puffed up to twice its normal size.

"YOU THINK YOU SCARE ME?" yelled David, swapping his stick for an even bigger one. "I'VE GOT SCARIER BEARS IN MY TOY COLLECTION! COME ANY CLOSER AND I'LL KNOCK THE STUFFING OUT OF YOU!"

The bear roared and charged forward. To the girls' horror, David also roared and charged forward. "LEMME ATCHA, TEDDY-BRAIN!" he yelled.

The bear slowed down and stopped. It had never encountered such an aggressive human before. It paused for a moment, as if weighing its options, then swiftly turned tail and fled into the trees.

"HAHAHA!" yelled David. "THAT'S RIGHT, RUN, YOU FURRY-FACED COWARD!"

The children continued along the path. The ground underfoot was soft and squelchy, and mangrove trees grew all around.

"Watch your step," warned Hilda. "I think we're coming to a swamp."

"I'm not scared of a silly swamp," said David. "No swamp can bog me down."

Hilda sighed. David used to be quite good company, but this new David was becoming unbearable.

The trees thinned and the children emerged into a wide swampy clearing dotted with bog cotton, fetterbushes, and water lilies. Out of the middle of the swamp rose a pyramid of huge, rectangular rocks.

"The Screaming Stones," breathed Hilda.

"They don't seem to be screaming," observed Frida. "Maybe they only scream at night."

David shrugged off his backpack and strode down into the swamp, waving his big stick high in the air. "Start screaming, then!" he cried. "We came a long way for this!"

Hilda dropped her backpack next to David's, picked up Twig and cautiously entered the swamp, testing its depth with every step. At first it only came up to her ankles but soon it was up to her knees. As she walked, she tried not to think of the pus spiders, rag leeches, and swamp toads described in *Swamps and Their Unfriendly Occupants*.

David stood waist deep in the swamp, swatting the stones with his stick. "Scream, curse you!" he cried. "I want to hear some Grade A screaming or I'll really give you something to scream about."

"David, be polite," said Hilda. She waded toward him, feeling the clutch of cool, thick mud around her legs. Twig suddenly went tense in her arms, staring at a patch of boggy ground to the right of the stones.

Hilda saw straight away what Twig had noticed—a bubble of air forming on the surface of the swamp. It swelled to the size of a football and then burst, splashing its surroundings with little flecks of mud. A second bubble swelled and burst, and then a sudden movement deep down in the bog caused a series of eerie ripples and shivers on top.

"There's something in there," said Hilda. She strode toward David, grabbed the stick out of his hand and pulled him behind the pile of stones.

"Hey!" cried David. "What are you—"

"Shhh," hissed Hilda.

Frida quickly joined them and they huddled together in the shadow of the stones as the swamp continued to bubble and ripple. Great swathes of mud and vegetation rose up out of the depths, knotting and clumping together to form what could only be described as a gigantic swamp man.

The creature's lanky arms and legs were shrouded in algae. Bog cotton stalks protruded from its shoulder blades and its oblong slab of a head was covered in purple filchweed. The children craned their necks as they watched the swamp man wade onto dry land and stalk off into the forest. It moved with a loping gait, as if its head was too heavy for its elongated body.

"Whoa," said Hilda. "I don't remember Emil Gammelplassen mentioning THAT in his book. I wonder what it's up to."

"I'll find out," said David, striding through the bog in pursuit of the swamp man. "I'll find out with my fists!"

"No!" Hilda took off after David and pushed him head-first into the mud. "I'm sorry David, but if you carry on acting this way, you'll put us all in danger."

"I'm not scared of danger," said David through a mouthful of mud.

"Well you should be," said Hilda. "Now, if you don't mind, we're going to follow that creature at a safe distance and see what he does."

By the time they all got up onto dry land, the swamp man was already out of sight. Twig, however, was an excellent tracker. He scurried forward through the trees, sniffing at bits of mud and vegetation, and the girls followed behind.

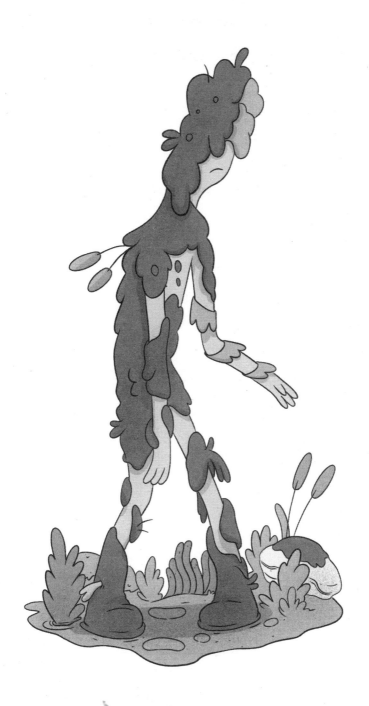

Hilda put an arm around David's shoulder as they walked. "David, you're not yourself," she said gently. "What exactly happened last night?"

"Nothing much," said David, "except that I bid goodbye to the enemy that has been holding me back my whole life. An enemy whose name begins with F."

Frida scowled. "I hope you don't mean me."

"Of course not," David said. "You're my friend. I'm talking about fear."

David told the girls about his meeting with the Vikings and his adventures on the battlefield. "You should have seen it," he concluded. "By the time the morning star rose in the east, not a single enemy warrior was left in one piece. My friend Torgund plucked the Medallion of Sigurd from Knudsen's lifeless body and we all leaned forward to touch it. As my fingers made contact with the cool metal, I felt a rush of power and confidence through my whole body, and hey presto, all my fears were gone!"

"Impossible," said Frida. "There haven't been Vikings around here for hundreds of years."

An anxious yap came from a clearing in the trees ahead.

"What is it, Twig?" said Hilda. "What have you found?"

They hurried out of the woods and found Twig cowering on the edge of a field. Hilda and Frida surveyed the scene and immediately understood why Twig was so upset.

6

Dozens of heads, bodies, arms, and legs were strewn across the battlefield. Many of the heads still wore their helmets.

Hilda gaped at David. "This was the battle you were in?"

"Yes." David shrugged. "It's not as bad as it looks, though. Everyone on my side survived."

Frida pointed at a huge, dark figure moving among the bodies.

"Look," she said. "It's Swamp Man."

The swamp man knelt down by one of the corpses and repositioned its head and limbs. Once all the body parts were in their correct places, the creature opened a small green vial and splashed a few drops of liquid onto the body.

The slain warrior yawned and sat bolt upright.

"Gah!" cried Hilda. "Did you see that?"

The swamp man moved on to another corpse and did the same again. One by one, the fallen warriors stirred their limbs and came back to life.

"This can't be real," said Frida, pinching herself.

"It's real all right." David sounded annoyed. "That silly oaf is undoing our great victory. I must go and tell Torgund."

"Don't!" cried Hilda. "He'll only want to fight them again."

But David was already dashing back into the woods. He stomped through thick nettle bushes, leaped over fallen branches and ran through giant cobwebs without even squealing. Normally, Hilda would have been able to beat David in a race, but this new, courageous David was faster than the old one and seemed to have no thought for his own safety. He reached Torgund's cave thirty yards ahead of Hilda, and fifty yards ahead of Frida.

Torgund was tucking into a bowl of sticky chicken wings when David skidded to a halt in front of him and blurted out the news: "It's Knudsen and his men! They're alive again! I've seen them with my own eyes!"

The Warrior of Thunder choked on a chicken bone and had to be saved by three hard slaps on the back from one-eyed Olaf. "How dare those ingrates come back to life," he spluttered, "especially after we gave them such honorable deaths? It's an insult, that's what it is! Prepare for battle, men! We can't let Knudsen reclaim the medallion."

The Vikings grabbed their weapons and charged out of the cave, hardly even noticing a blue-haired girl coming in the other direction.

"Hey!" called Hilda, as they knocked her to the ground. "Why not just keep your medallion and go home? Wouldn't that be fun?"

The warriors paid no attention. They charged on into the forest, shrieking wild war cries to the wind.

Frida appeared at Hilda's side. "Are you all right?"

Hilda got to her feet and brushed herself down. "Got a bit trampled there," she said, "but such is the life of an adventurer. Where's David?"

"He went with the Vikings."

"Oh, no!" cried Hilda. "We need to stop him before he gets hurt."

With Twig at their heels, they dashed back through the forest. When they arrived at the battlefield, they saw that Knudsen's warriors had formed a siege formation in the middle of the battlefield, their shields interlocked like the shell of an enormous tortoise.

Hilda looked for David, and saw him staggering toward the tortoise formation with a sword that was far too big for him. She caught up to him and grabbed him by the collar.

"David, stop!" she shrieked. "You'll be killed."

"That's just fear talking!" he retorted.

"Exactly," said Hilda, "and fear can be a good thing! Use your eyes, David. The fearless side is getting slaughtered. They need a bit of fear to make them fight smart."

"No, they don't!" cried David. "They just need ME to help them!"

David squirmed free of Hilda's grasp and charged toward the tortoise formation, waving his giant sword aloft. By the time he reached the

Knudsen shields, his arm was already exhausted.

"David!" shrieked Hilda.

It was too late. As Hilda and Frida looked on in horror, one of Knudsen's men burst out of the defensive formation, lopped off David's head and retreated gleefully behind the wall of shields.

Hilda and Frida screamed again and again as David's headless body fumbled around in the mud, searching for his head.

"This is all my fault," wept Hilda. "If I hadn't told that story about the razorbeak eagle, David would have stayed in the tent last night. And if I hadn't suggested following the swamp man, we'd be halfway home by now."

"That's it!" cried Frida. "The swamp man! If anyone can put David back together, he can!"

They ran back to the swamp and arrived just in time to see the swamp man rising up out of the bog.

"Swamp Man!" yelled Frida.

"My name's Sigurd,' said the creature. "You wouldn't like it if I called you Flesh Girl, would you?"

"Sorry," said Hilda, "but our friend needs your help. He got his head cut off, you see."

Sigurd heaved a weary sigh. "Calm down," he said. "I'll take care of it, like I do every night."

"Are you saying they do this every night? How long has it been going on?"

"Feels like forever," said Sigurd.

"And you keep saving them?"

A watery chuckle bubbled up from the swamp creature's throat. "I'm not saving them," he said. "I'm getting back at them. Those Vikings stole my medallion from me. And another clan stole it from them. I'm getting back at them all by making them fight for it every single night."

"So the screaming we heard last night was... "

"Battlefield screaming."

"We thought it was the stones."

"My rock collection?" Sigurd looked amazed. "Of course not. Everybody knows that rocks don't scream."

Hilda felt very silly, and also rather annoyed at Emil Gammelplassen. He was still her favorite author but he should not have jumped to conclusions about the Screaming Stones.

"Sigurd," said Frida. "Why don't you take your medallion back?"

Sigurd considered this for a long time, then shook his head. "Nah," he said. "That thing just makes you an idiot. I'd rather continue my prank."

"I don't think I like your prank," said Hilda. "It seems a bit cruel."

Sigurd's shoulders slumped. "Perhaps you're right," he said. "Perhaps I should put an end to it."

He heaved himself out of the swamp and led the way back to the battlefield. The screaming had stopped and the bodies of Torgund's army lay all around. David's body sat in the middle of the field and his head still wore an expression of surprised displeasure.

"Do you want to do the honors?" said Sigurd, passing Hilda his magic green vial.

"My friend will do it," said Hilda, passing the vial to Frida. "She's good with magic potions."

7

Frida put David's head back on and sprinkled potion on his neck from the magic vial. As soon as David woke up, Twig bounded forward and nuzzled him affectionately.

"Where am I?" said David. "The last thing I remember was running away from the tent and falling down a hill. I'm such a scaredy-cat!"

"Don't worry," said Hilda, ruffling his hair. "We like you being a scaredy-cat."

"That's right, said Frida. "Someone's got to talk sense into us from time to time."

David smiled, then noticed the dead bodies all around and the swamp creature scowling down at him. "Argh!" David sprang to his feet and backed away. "Aieee!" He tripped over an obstacle and lay sprawled on the ground. "AAAARGH!" He realized that the obstacle was in fact a cheerful-looking head without a body.

"Don't worry, David," said Hilda. "Sigurd is going to revive all of your Vikings one last time. And as for us, we're going to fetch our backpacks and head straight home. How does that sound?"

"Sounds good," said David in a sheepish voice.

"Hi Mom, I'm home!" yelled Hilda, bursting in through the front door and kicking off her boots.

"Hilda!" Mom must have heard Hilda's footsteps on the stairs because she was already standing in the corridor with a displeased expression on her face.

"Wow, that smells good," said Hilda. "You've got a pie in the oven, haven't you? Let me guess. Leek and potato? Spinach and rowanberry?"

"Remind me, Hilda, what time did you promise to be home by?"

"Er... I'm not sure."

"Lunchtime," said Mom.

"Oh."

"So when lunchtime came and went, I called Frida's mom to ask her where you were."

"Oh."

"And what do you think Frida's mom said? I'll tell you what she said. SHE SAID SHE THOUGHT FRIDA WAS AT OUR HOUSE!"

"Oh."

"STOP SAYING OH AND TELL ME WHERE YOU'VE BEEN!"

"We went camping," said Hilda.

"CAMPING! CAMPING WHERE?"

"At the castle."

"AT THE CASTLE? THE CASTLE OUTSIDE THE CITY WALLS! HILDA, WHAT HAVE I TOLD YOU ABOUT GOING OUTSIDE THE CITY WALLS? YOU KNOW HOW DANGEROUS IT IS OUT THERE! DON'T YOU REMEMBER WHAT THE COMMANDER OF THE TROLBERG SAFETY PATROL SAID ON THE NEWS YESTERDAY?"

"No," said Hilda, who was no fan of Commander Erik Ahlberg.

"He said there have been more troll fires than ever burning around Trolberg these last few nights."

"Maybe the trolls have discovered the joys of camping."

"An 'alarming increase', that's what he called it—and you were out there in the middle of them!"

"Yes, I was," said Hilda. "Happy and free, for one night only."

"And what's that supposed to mean?"

Hilda could contain herself no longer. "It means I'd rather be out there with the trolls than cooped up in this apartment!"

"Right, that's enough." Mom's voice shook with powerful emotion. "Hilda, you're grounded."

"What?" Hilda stared at Mom and her eyes prickled with tears.

"Extremely grounded," said Mom. "No going out. No friends. No adventures. You are not leaving this apartment until I say so."

Hilda could bear it no longer. She grabbed

Twig, stormed to her room and slammed the door so hard that the frame shuddered on its hinges.

"You should be careful what you wish for," said a stern voice, and a fuzzy head poked out from underneath the bed. "You're lucky, Hilda. You have a warm, cozy home and a mom who loves you."

Hilda threw her toy woff at the house spirit, missing his head by a whisker. "I meant every word I said," she snapped. "I do wish I was out there with the trolls. In fact, I wish I was troll."

A sudden bang sounded from one of the troll fires on the mountainside, casting an eerie, orange flash across the bedroom wall.

"Tontu, I need to use Nowhere Space to get to Frida's house," said Hilda suddenly. "Frida is practicing her invisibility spell tonight, and I should be there to help her. I'm her familiar, after all."

"No way," said Tontu. "For one thing, Nowhere Space is for essential travel only. For another, Mom is baking a pie tonight."

"Fine." Hilda narrowed her eyes. "But what if I told Mom that she didn't lose her favorite bowl?

What if I told her that you broke it and hid the evidence in your hidey-hole?"

Tontu considered this. "All right," he said. "Take my hand."

Hilda reached for Tontu's hand and at that exact moment, Mom came into the room.

"Pie's ready Hilda, so if you're hungry, you might as well come and—HILDA!" Mom ran to grab Hilda's free hand. "Don't you dare go in there, young lady!"

Hilda doubled her grip on Tontu's hand. She was already halfway into Nowhere Space but Mom was trying to pull her back.

"Let go of me!" shrieked Hilda.

"You come back here this minute!" cried Mom.

Mom and Tontu pulled Hilda this way and that. One moment it seemed as if all three of them were about to tumble into Nowhere Space, the next it seemed they would all end up in a heap on Hilda's bedroom carpet. The pressure on Hilda's arms was becoming unbearable.

"Hilda, this is really dangerous!" yelled Tontu. "If you don't come all the way through, you could end up being catapulted into lim—"

It was already too late. Hilda's ears popped and she felt a strange, falling sensation as she flipped head over heels into the dank, cavernous nothingness of limbo. The worst thing about limbo was the fact that it was completely airless. As Hilda fell, she winced and squirmed, trying desperately to breathe.

Then, POOSH! In a dazzling flash of light, Hilda shot out of limbo, fell onto something hard, rolled down a rocky slope and stopped at the bottom in a painful tangle of arms and legs.

A moment later, Mom fell right on top of her. Twig, too, because he had been hanging on to Mom's pant leg.

Mother and daughter rolled apart and lay side by side on the rocky surface, sucking in deep lungfuls of air and blinking in astonishment.

Hilda was first to recover. "Mom!" she cried, hugging her. "Are you OK?"

"I don't know yet." Mom touched her back and winced. "Is this Nowhere Space?"

Hilda got to her feet and looked around her.

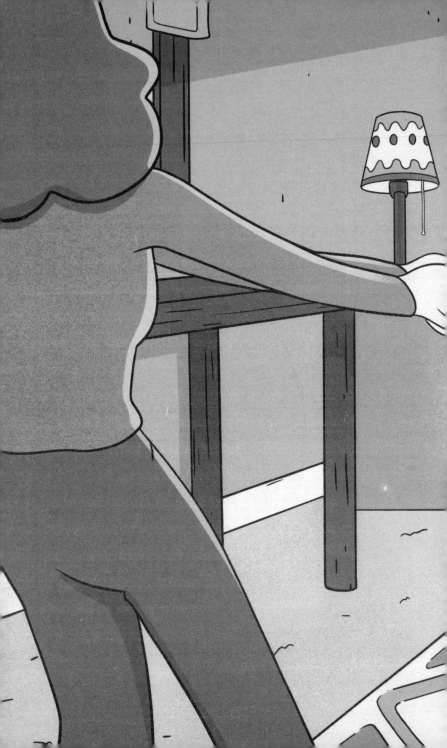

The landscape was dark and desolate. All around them loomed giant tree trunks that looked like they were made of stone.

"Doesn't look like Nowhere Space," said Hilda, walking off among the trees. "Something went wrong and it seems to have catapulted us to who knows where."

"We should stay here and wait for Tontu," said Mom. "If we wander off, we'll only get lost."

"We're already lost," said Hilda. "And there's no point waiting for Tontu. He could be on the other side of the world for all we know."

They reached a ledge and looked out over another vast, gloomy expanse of rocks and stony tree trunks. There was no breeze at all. It was the strangest place that Hilda had ever been in.

"Come on," said Mom. "I saw some flattish rocks back there—we can get some sleep."

8

As the sun rose over Trolberg, David was woken up by a frantic knocking on his bedroom window. He jumped in fright, then recognized the tiny figure on the outside window sill.

"Alfur!" He opened the window for the little elf. "I haven't seen you in ages."

"Something terrible has happened," gabbled Alfur, removing his pointy hat. "I got back from the northern counties this morning and you'll never guess what I found on the table in Hilda's apartment."

David paled. "A nightmare spirit?"

"Worse."

"A troll?"

"Worse," squealed Alfur. "A pie!"

"What?"

"Who bakes a delicious spinach and rowanberry pie, sets the table for dinner, puts the pie in the middle of the table, and then just leaves it there?"

"Weird," agreed David.

"And here's another thing." Alfur lowered his voice to an ominous whisper. "I spoke to a messenger elf who told me that he happened to pass by Hilda's window last night, and he says he heard her shout that she intended to go and live with the trolls out in the wilderness."

"Really?" David scratched his head. "That doesn't sound like Hilda."

"It sounds exactly like Hilda!" said Alfur.

"You think she's run away?"

"Yes, I do. And Mom's bed hasn't been slept in either, which means she must have gone searching for Hilda. So what are we going to do?"

David frowned. "Let's call Frida," he said at last, "and do whatever she suggests."

Frida agreed with Alfur about the most likely explanation for this strange course of events. She told Alfur to wait in Hilda's apartment in case someone returned. Meanwhile, she and David would head out into the wilderness as a search party.

They biked to the edge of the Great Forest, as before, and hid their bikes in giant roffleworts, as before. As they ventured into the forest, Frida saw a forest giant lumbering among the trees, and three plump troll rocks sitting around the blackened remains of a campfire.

Late in the afternoon, a woff emerged from a hollow bludbok tree, dipped down beside them as if in greeting, then soared high up into the air.

"Look!" cried Frida, beside herself with excitement.

It was not unusual to see woffs in the wilderness. Every few days they migrated down the valley in great flocks, their fluffy tails flickering from side to side and their huge eyes staring straight ahead. But this woff was unusual for two reasons. First, it was alone. Second, it was not yellow like a normal woff. It was dazzling white.

Frida smiled as she watched the beautiful creature. "When the white woff flies, the witches smile," she whispered. "Must be a good month for magic."

A shadow fell across the forest and an immense dirigible floated into view above the treetops.

"Look who's here," said Frida, pointing at the Safety Patrol logo on the side of the airship. "As if we didn't have enough problems already."

"Oh no!" cried David. "The white woff is heading straight toward it!"

He was right. The woff seemed to be flying on a direct collision course with the dirigible. Any second now, and that beautiful, magical creature was going to get knocked out of the sky.

"Hey!" screamed Frida, jumping and waving. "Look out!"

As the woff neared the dirigible, the control pod hanging underneath the airship banked

suddenly to starboard, as if the pilot had tugged the joystick violently to the right. Like a speeding arrow, the woff flew straight and true between the metal struts of the pod, and on into the vast blue sky beyond.

"Bravo!" cried Frida. "How's that for an evasive manoeuvre?"

But she had spoken too soon. Humungous airships are not designed for aerobatics, and the sudden jolt seemed to have thrown the aircraft off balance. It banked and swung from side to side, lurching and staggering like a drunken giant, the control pod nosing further and further down until it brushed the topmost leaves of the lofty iron pines. Frida saw the pilot, Safety Patrol deputy Gerda Gustav, hunched over the controls in the cockpit, her face pale and drawn.

"They've lost control!" yelled David. "Come on, Gerda. Pull up! Pull up!"

The mighty aircraft did pull up, inch by precious inch, its nose straining upward into the sky. But just as it seemed to be out of danger, its tail end clipped the tip of a sturdy iron pine, puncturing the canvas balloon full of pressurized gas. An eerie hissing sound echoed among the trees and the dirigible went wild, zooming all over the place like a leaping, swooping, fast-deflating party balloon.

Frida and David screamed as the zeppelin came crashing down through the branches and skidded along the ground toward them.

"RUN!" shrieked Frida, grabbing David's hand and sprinting down the track. The zeppelin ploughed after them, smashing through the undergrowth. Frida glanced back and saw that Erik Ahlberg had joined Gerda Gustav in the cockpit. There he stood, hanging on to the back of the pilot's chair, white-knuckled and bug-eyed with fear.

The zeppelin slowed down and came to a stop. A flock of startled starlings flew up into the sky as the nose of the airship crumpled against a mighty iron pine trunk.

Frida and David stopped running and turned to stare at the wreckage. The door of the control pod creaked open and Ahlberg stumbled out. His feathered hat was still on his head but his eyes were dazed and unfocused.

"Never fear, children!" Ahlberg cried. "You're safe with me."

Gerda Gustav appeared behind him, pushing him away from the wrecked airship.

"Everybody back!" she yelled. "Go, go, go! Back behind that rock!"

As soon as he realized the danger he was in, Ahlberg put on a surprising turn of speed. He barged past Frida, knocking her to the ground, and threw himself behind the granite boulder. David and Gerda rushed to Frida's aid. They seized one arm each, dragged her behind the rock, and ducked down low.

They all shut their eyes tight and clung to each other as a deafening boom rocked the forest. Tongues of fire singed their hair and eyebrows, and plumes of acrid smoke made them cough and splutter.

When the smoke cleared, David craned his neck to look back at the zeppelin. It had exploded in a ball of fire, flinging bits of wreckage all over the forest floor, and now it was quietly burning itself out.

Frida touched her foot and winced. "I think I've sprained my ankle," she said.

9

Mom and Hilda trudged through the silent
forest with Twig at their heels. On a walk in the
wilderness, Twig would normally have rushed
ahead to sniff the flowers and paw at insects, but
in this strange, gloomy landscape he seemed tense
and anxious, as if sensing danger all around.
Besides, there were no flowers or insects here, nor
any color at all, just mile upon mile of slate gray
tree trunks and boulders.

There was barely enough light to see where
they were going, let alone to see the tops of the

trees, which towered into nothingness above their heads. They had woken up at ten o'clock that morning, according to Mom's watch, and now it was two in the afternoon. "Why is it still dark?" they kept asking each other, but neither of them had any answer for that.

"If you had only listened to me..." said Mom for the hundredth time.

"If you hadn't grabbed my hand..." replied Hilda, exasperated.

They had not drunk anything since yesterday, and their thirst was making them tetchy. They sat down on the ground, leaning against a tree trunk, and Twig nuzzled their legs, trying in vain to keep their spirits up.

"At least we're together," said Mom.

"Yes," said Hilda.

The trunk felt hard and cold against Hilda's back. Not like a real tree at all, she thought. It's almost as if this whole forest is made of stone.

They were quiet for a long time, each lost in their own thoughts, and then Hilda felt Mom's body suddenly tense.

"What is it?" she whispered.

"There's something on my hand," hissed Mom.

Ever so slowly Mom raised her hand in front of her face and peered through the darkness at the thing on her hand. When she saw it, she screamed and flicked her hand to shake it off. Twig jumped to his feet, braced for a fight.

"It's all right," said Mom, making an effort to sound calm. "Some sort of disgusting slug, that's all."

"Great," said Hilda, who was not afraid of slugs, disgusting or otherwise. "I was beginning to think we were the only living things in this place."

Mom stood up. "Let's keep going," she said. "We really need to find water."

She strode off, but Hilda rushed after her and pulled her back. "Mom!"

"What is it?" snapped Mom.

"You were about to walk into a ravine," said Hilda.

Mom shuddered as she peered into the chasm at her feet. "Whoops," she said. "Thanks, Hilda."

Hilda wanted to try jumping across the ravine,

but Mom stopped her. So they turned and walked along it instead, eyes on the ground, their footsteps echoing in the darkness.

Half a mile further on, a large, flat boulder had been laid across the ravine, forming a bridge. As Hilda walked across, she could not help wondering who or what had hauled that boulder into place.

On the other side of the ravine, Hilda spotted a dark pool that looked like it could be water. She ran to it and plunged her hands into the cool liquid.

"Yes!" she shouted, and was about to cup her hand to her mouth, when Mom stopped her. "Don't drink that, Hilda. It's stagnant."

Hilda nearly wept in frustration, but the discovery of water had made Mom hopeful. "Cheer up," she said. "It must have come from somewhere. All we have to do is listen carefully for the sound of—aha!"

Hilda heard it, too, the unmistakable sound of running water. They set off toward it, scrambling over boulders and splashing through rock pools. The sound grew louder all the time and Hilda's

heart flooded with hope. "That's more than just a stream, Mom! That's a waterfall!"

A huge pile of boulders blocked their path. Slim rays of light shone out between the boulders. Hilda squeezed through a narrow gap, then reached back in and pulled Mom after her.

"Tight squeeze," grinned Mom. "You'd better pull hard…" Her voice trailed off and her eyes widened as she took in her surroundings.

"What?" said Hilda, turning to look. "Oh," she added. "Wow."

The vast space they found themselves in was more cavern than forest, and the trees were not in fact trees but huge pillars of stone stretching all the way up to a ceiling of rock at least a hundred yards above their heads. The source of the light was a hole in the ceiling, through which a magnificent cascade of water plummeted into a plunge pool. Rays of light refracting through the tumbling water formed a glorious double rainbow in the mist above the pool.

But Hilda and Mom were not alone in the cavern. Far from it. Wherever Hilda looked, she saw trolls of every shape and size. Some splashed in the plunge pool or the streams that flowed from it. Some sat on boulders gazing at the waterfall. Some snored. Some argued. Some wrestled.

"I don't believe it," breathed Mom. "I've never heard of so many trolls all in one place."

Hilda opened her mouth to speak but her throat was so parched with thirst that her voice came out as a dust-dry croak. "Me neither."

"There's another of those horrible slugs," said Mom, pointing.

The slug was making its way along a slab of stone near Hilda's left elbow. As she looked at it, the slug opened its jaws and chomped down hard on the stone, taking a big bite out of it.

"Rock-eating slugs," croaked Hilda. "I think *Caves and Their Unfriendly Occupants* mentioned something about those."

"Look there," Mom whispered, pointing to a rivulet of fresh water that snaked away from the plunge pool behind a row of high boulders.

"Maybe that would be a good spot to drink."

They scuttled from boulder to boulder, terrified of being spotted, and at last they found themselves in a safe, secluded spot, hidden from the view of the lounging trolls. They knelt down by the stream and scooped crystal-clear water into their mouths, gulping it gratefully until they could drink no more.

"That's better," said Hilda, wiping her mouth with the back of her hand, but at that moment she felt the grip of strong teeth on her pant-leg, hauling her away from the stream into the shadow of a boulder.

"What is it, Twig?" she whispered. "What's wrong?"

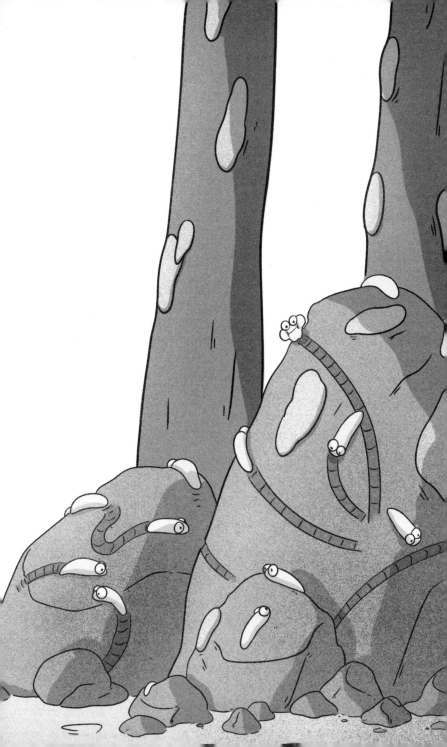

10

Hilda soon had her answer. Peering around the side of the boulder, she saw an enormous troll emerge from a nearby cave. A tiny troll child waddled at its side, followed by a sorry-looking goat on the end of a rope. Piled up on the goat's back was an enormous bundle of provisions: three sacks, a barrel, a leg of meat, and an enormous clump of what looked like radishes.

Mom had seen it, too. She darted to Hilda's side and flattened herself against the boulder, holding her breath. A sudden chomping sound made Hilda jump, but it was just another rock-eating slug.

The bigger troll, presumably the troll child's mother, looked left and right and sniffed the air. She growled softly at the back of her throat, and lumbered over to the boulder where Hilda and Mom were hiding.

"Ba ba ba ba baba," said a high-pitched voice, and Hilda turned away from the mother troll to see the troll child standing right in front of her, babbling excitedly.

"Shhhh," urged Mom. "Shhh shh!"

"Ba babababa!" laughed the child, pointing at Twig.

The mother troll plodded round the boulder to see what her baby was pointing at. She looked down at the three non-troll intruders, and for a moment she seemed as shocked as they were. Then her maternal instincts took over and she let out a terrifying roar that echoed off the rocky walls and ceiling of the vast cavern.

Hilda jumped aside as the mother troll's fist slammed down beside her. "RUN!" cried Mom, and off they shot, splashing through rock pools and clambering over boulders, their footfalls slapping loudly on the rocky ground. The mother troll pursued them, roaring her displeasure, her rancid breath warm on the back of Hilda's neck.

The goat flashed past in front of them, its rope-leash dangling free and its heavy bundle swaying precariously as it ran.

"Follow that goat!" cried Mom, grabbing Hilda's hand and dragging her after the stricken animal, through a series of labyrinthine passageways. This way, that way, this way, that way, left and right and right again, Hilda had no idea her Mom could run so fast.

Perhaps Mom thought that the goat knew a way out of this nightmarish cavern. Perhaps she imagined that it would lead them to freedom and that the four of them would live happily ever after as one strange but happy family: mother, daughter, deer fox, and goat.

Whatever Mom might have thought, she thought wrong. The goat led them to the deadest of dead ends, a complete cul-de-sac surrounded on three sides by high, smooth walls of solid granite.

The goat skidded to a halt and looked back mournfully. It gave an apologetic little bleat, as if to say: I'm sorry, truly I am, but I'm only a goat. You should not have trusted your lives to my sense of direction.

A few seconds later, the mother troll also rounded the corner. There before her was her goat, still bearing its precious bundle of food, but the two humans and the deer fox had inexplicably disappeared. The only living things in sight were the goat, the troll child, and a dozen rock-eating slugs.

Back in the Great Forest, near the wreck of the Safety Patrol dirigible, Frida leaned against a boulder, nursing her sprained ankle.

Erik Ahlberg sat opposite her, talking about trolls.

"If you had seen what I saw from the air today," he said, "the blood in your veins would turn to ice. I counted hundreds of troll fires dotted all over the mountainsides and the Great Forest, and as you know, hundreds is practically thousands, which is very nearly a million. Horrific, when you think about it. I'm supposed to go on *Trolberg Tonight* to report on the results of today's mission, but I'm guessing we're not going to make it back in time for tonight's show. Don't worry, child, it's not your fault. Such an injury could have happened to any untrained individual."

"You tripped me," said Frida coldly.

"I saved you," shot back Ahlberg. "A little gratitude would be nice."

A cry of excitement filled the air and David and Gerda emerged from the trees carrying a large, black crate between them.

"The emergency supplies box survived the crash!" beamed Gerda. "It contains a first-aid pack, three days' rations, and a blimp kit."

"What's a blimp?" asked Frida.

"A tiny aircraft," said Ahlberg. "That little beauty is going to fly us right out of here. It only takes three hours to build."

"But the sun is already going down," said David, "and we're surrounded by troll rocks."

Ahlberg puffed out his chest and flicked the feather in his hat. "You three build the blimp," he said, "and I'll take care of the trolls! How does that sound?"

"Terrifying," muttered David.

Gerda found the blimp assembly instructions and laid out the pieces on the charred grass. There were ropes, fiberglass poles and dozens of mysterious metal components. While Gerda busied herself with the blimp, David found a bandage in the first aid kit, and wrapped Frida's ankle.

"Good job," smiled Frida, turning her foot this way and that to admire David's handiwork.

"First Aid was my very first Sparrow Scout badge," said David. "I also know what to do if you get bitten by a snaggletooth python..." He looked anxious and peered into the long grass behind him.

"I'm sure that won't happen," said Frida. "Come on, let's help Gerda build the blimp."

Making a passenger basket out of the bendy poles was easy enough, but the motor was fiendishly difficult. The instructions said to attach the flange to the crankshaft, but none of them knew what those words meant. As for David, he kept glancing apprehensively at the balloon itself, which was flatpacked into a canvas bag covered with yellow and black warning symbols. The words on the side were hardly reassuring.

"TO INFLATE, PULL RIPCORD AND RETREAT AT LEAST TEN PACES."

The sun set behind Mount Halldór and one by one the stars came out. From the mountains all around them came the eerie sound of rocks cracking and re-structuring.

"David, could you shine a flashlight on this for me?" said Frida, who was dexterously attaching what she hoped was a flange to what she imagined might be a crankshaft.

"Sure." David hurried over to her.

The sounds from the mountainside were now more animal than mineral, a cacophony of yawning, growling, and lip-smacking.

David's hand trembled more than ever. "Sorry," he said again, grabbing the flashlight in both hands.

There was a sudden crack of branches close at hand and two wrestling trolls rolled out of the bushes right in front of them. Two more followed. They grinned when they saw the gaggle of human beings goggling up at them.

"Take it easy, everyone," whispered Gerda. "Whatever you do, don't antagonize them."

Commander Ahlberg had other ideas. He ran

straight at the trolls, waving and shouting.
"Back, you beasts!" he cried. "I'll have your guts
for garters!"

The trolls surrounded Ahlberg and circled him,
grinning and drooling. One of them curled its
hand into a colossal fist.

"Please!" cried Gerda to the trolls. "Don't
harm him!"

Ahlberg's initial burst of bravery quickly wore
off and he realized the danger he was in. He
tried to dart out of the circle of trolls, but they
kept moving to block his way. One grabbed his
feathered hat and placed it on its own head at a
jaunty angle.

Frida had an idea. She delved in her shoulder
bag and pulled out a small pouch—the dust she
had collected at the ruined castle. She poured
some of the dust into her palm and crept toward
the trolls. She began to chant the spell:
"Lund Skipta..."

On the last word—"Kvinkindi!"—she threw the
dust into the middle of the circle of trolls. Erik
Ahlberg spluttered and his head transformed into

that of a giant insect. The trolls stared in horror at his huge bug eyes, his hideous mouthparts and his long, hairy antennae, waggling at them reproachfully.

Three of the trolls turned and fled, but the one in the hat reached out to touch the bewildered insect man.

POP! Erik Ahlberg completely disappeared.

The troll jumped backward as if it had been scalded, then turned and fled into the forest.

Frida was almost as surprised as the trolls had been. "It worked!" she cried. "My spell worked!"

"Did you see that?" The tiny, nasal voice seemed to come from somewhere on David's head. "Did you see how they ran from me?!"

Gerda and Frida peered at David's hair and there, just above his left ear, was a yellow and brown bug with a tiny Safety Patrol logo on its abdomen. It was waving four of its legs and cheering shrilly.

"Oh no," gasped Frida. "I must have done the chant wrong. I seem to have turned Mr Ahlberg into a bug."

11

The mother troll led her goat and her child out onto a ledge overlooking the Great Forest. She gazed up at the stars and sucked into her lungs a delicious mouthful of cool, fresh air.

The goat kept bleating plaintively and sinking down on its haunches, as if the weight of the bundle on its back was too much for it. If the mother troll had stopped to think about the goat's unusual behavior, she might have understood the mysterious disappearance of those two human beings she had chased through the mountain.

But she did not stop to think about it. She simply slapped the goat on its bottom to chivy it forward along the ledge.

A group of trolls was gathered around a bonfire under the starry sky. The mother troll reached into the bundle of provisions and pulled out three hunks of raw meat, a sack of grain, and a clump of radishes. The perfect distractions for unfriendly fellow trolls. She tossed it to the them and they began to devour the food, munching and gnawing and smacking their lips. The mother scooped up her child, made her way carefully down the slope, and joined the feast around the fire.

Hilda poked her head out from inside the bundle where she was hiding and took a deep breath. A big wooden barrel was digging painfully into her ribs, but she no longer cared about that, because for the first time that day she recognized her surroundings. She was out in the open air on the lower slopes of Boot Mountain. The Great Forest was spread out beneath her and there in the far distance, twinkling welcomingly, were the lights of Trolberg.

"Psst, Mom!" Hilda pulled her head back inside the bundle of provisions. "Turns out we were in Boot Mountain the whole time! I can see Trolberg! We just have to walk down the hill and we'll be home by morning!"

"Hilda, that's wonderful!" Mom raised her hand and they high-fived silently. "Is the coast clear? Can we make a run for it?"

"There's a group of trolls around the fire," whispered Hilda, "but they're busy eating. I don't think they'll notice us."

Hilda and Mom wriggled out of the bundle and dropped silently to the ground. Hilda pressed her body against the rock and moved forward in a low cat crawl. Mom followed, hardly daring to breathe.

"RAAAAARRRRRR!!!"

The sudden roar made Hilda jump. She looked up and saw a gigantic two-headed troll burst out of the opening in the mountain and charge to the bonfire where the other trolls were feasting. It snatched a meaty bone out of a furry troll's hand and chomped down on it.

The furry troll ran at the intruder and tackled it around its knees. Another troll jumped onto its back, another headbutted it in the midriff. But the colossal, two-headed troll was bigger and stronger than all of them. It punched and snapped and roared and slapped.

The mother troll snatched up her child and ran back into their cave. Hilda and Mom ran in the other direction, sprinting down the mountainside as fast as their legs would carry them, staggering and stumbling as they went, dodging flying rocks and bones. They no longer cared about stealth, only speed.

When they reached the foot of Boot Mountain, they leaped into the middle of a giant rofflewort and cowered there, clinging to each other and

panting heavily.

"Are we still in danger?" panted Mom. "Were any of them chasing us?"

"I don't think so," said Hilda.

She raised her head an inch or two and looked back up the mountain, just in time to see the two-headed troll pick up the last of its attackers and hurl it into a bush. The twin heads roared again—thunderous, full-blooded roars that shook the mountainside. Then it hoisted the goat and the bundle of food onto its left shoulder and disappeared into the cave.

"Phew," said Mom. "I wouldn't want to be on the wrong side of that thing."

Hilda giggled with relief. "It was kind of traumatic," she said. "But such is the life of an— OH NO!"

"What is it?"

"TWIG!" Hilda leaped out of the rofflewort and started to sprint back up the mountain.

"Hilda, wait!" Mom dashed after her and grabbed her by the shoulders. "I'm sure Twig's fine. He probably escaped a different way."

"He's not fine!" Hilda tried to wrest herself from her Mom's tight grip. "If he was fine, he'd be here. He's still in that bundle, I know he is. Maybe his antlers snagged on a sack of grain, or maybe he was wedged in too tightly and couldn't get out. The two-headed troll has got him, Mom! Don't you understand? I've got to go back!"

"You'll do no such thing!"

"But Mom, this is Twig we're talking about!" Hilda's tears were flowing freely now.

"Have you forgotten how many times he saved my life? Have you forgotten the razorbeak eagle? Twig left his family and came to save me, remember? I'm going back, and there's nothing you can do to—"

"Hilda!" Mom was on the brink of tears as well. "Listen to me! You're not going back for Twig. I am."

Hilda stared at Mom. She had not expected that.

"I mean it," said Mom. "I'll go in there, I'll find Twig, and I'll bring him back to you, okay? And you are going to stay right here and wait for me."

"But—"

"No buts, Hilda." Mom's voice was stern. "You get inside that rofflewort and you stay there, understand?"

Hilda wiped her cheeks with the back of her hand and nodded silently. Then she watched, astonished, as Mom clambered back up the north side of Boot Mountain and disappeared into the cave.

12

On the south side of Boot Mountain, on the edge
of the Great Forest, Gerda, Frida, and David
huddled together, shivering with cold. Frida's
bandaged ankle was stretched out in front of her,
and David cradled a Thermos in his lap. Above
them stretched the wide night sky, inexpressibly
vast, bisected by a bright strip of stars which the
ancients knew as the Road of Milk.

Gerda had decided that with so many trolls on
the move, it was too dangerous to finish building
the blimp. Their own safety should be the priority,

she had said. They had covered the half-assembled blimp with iron pine branches and gone looking for a good hiding place. After a few minutes, they had found a secluded spot surrounded by rocks and ferns.

"Are you sure that Commander Ahlberg is all right in there?" asked Gerda for the hundredth time.

David unscrewed the top of his Thermos flask and listened. "Sounds fine to me," he said, putting the top back on. "Alive and buzzing."

"How about you?" Gerda asked Frida.
"Are you okay?"

"Ankle feels fine," said Frida, her teeth
chattering. "But I'm so c-c-cold."

"We should make a fire," said David.
"Remember what you said the other night, Frida?
There are so many troll fires around Trolberg these
days, one more won't make a difference."

He busied himself collecting twigs and branches
for the fire. Gerda found a box of matches in the
emergency supplies box, and soon they had a good
blaze going.

"Hey Gerda," said David. "You mentioned
something about emergency rations?"

Gerda grinned. "Do you like Jorts?"

"Do bears like honey?" laughed David. "Of
course I like Jorts!"

They opened a packet of Jorts and passed
it around, taking one at a time. The Jorts were
flavorful and salty, the perfect camping snack.

"So, tell me," said Gerda. "What were you
doing outside the wall?"

"Our friend ran away from home," said Frida.

"Her Mom went missing, too. We heard they'd come out here."

"I'm sorry to hear that," said Gerda, and she sounded genuinely concerned. "Why didn't you go to the authorities?"

Frida shrugged. "They're not very helpful most of the time."

Gerda stared into the fire and nodded sadly. "Point taken," she whispered.

All three of them were silent for a while, warming their hands against the fire, lost in thought. David thought of Hilda and wondered where she was right now. Wherever she was, he hoped that at least she was safe and warm.

There was a sudden rustle in the bushes and a troll stepped into the firelight. It lumbered forward, staring at the terrified campers, and the terrified campers stared right back.

David was the first to recover his composure. Something clicked in his brain and a memory came back to him. A memory of feeling different. A memory of feeling fearless.

David saw his hand stretch out in front of him and he heard himself greet the troll in a weirdly casual voice. "Hello there. Would you like a Jort?"

The troll kept eye contact with David as it leaned forward and sniffed the Jorts. Then it grabbed the whole bag and plumped itself down by the fire.

"Well," whispered Frida, forcing a smile. "This is cozy, isn't it?"

The troll downed all the Jorts in one go and slapped the empty bag upside-down on its head like a hat.

"Looking good," said David, approvingly.

The troll's body seemed to relax a little. It stared into the flames and sighed contentedly.

Hilda crouched in the middle of the giant rofflewort, staring at the cave entrance where Mom had disappeared. How long had it been now? Judging by the progress of the constellation Thor across the sky, it had been at least two hours.

"Sorry, Mom," Hilda whispered, "but that's all the waiting I can do."

She vaulted out of the rofflewort and hurried up Boot Mountain in a low crouch. All over the mountainside, troll fires crackled and hissed with wild energy. Hilda steered well clear of them, taking a long, zigzagging route.

At last she reached the abandoned fire near the mouth of the cave, the one where the group of trolls had feasted on meat and radishes. Hilda reached down and chose a good stick from the fire. It was about a foot long, burning brightly at one end.

Hilda dashed into the cave, holding her flaming torch low to the ground, eyes peeled for clues. She noticed a little pile of goat droppings halfway along the tunnel, and then another further on.

She came to a fork in the path, where three identical-looking tunnels snaked deep into the mountain. Which one to take? thought Hilda. Which one? Back and forth she shuffled, waving the flaming torch from side to side. Then she saw it: a tiny apple core lying in the mouth of the leftmost tunnel.

She picked it up and examined the tooth marks. Definitely human and deer-fox. Hilda had found the apple inside the troll's bundle of provisions, and she, Mom and Twig had taken a few bites each.

Hilda ran up the apple-core tunnel, following its twists and turns. A narrow path led down to her left and Hilda stopped again, unsure which way to go. There were no clues of any sort—until a muffled bleat rang out ahead.

The goat!

Holding the flaming torch ahead of her, Hilda ran full speed along the tunnel and found the entrance to a cave. Hefty bludbok logs had been lashed together to form a massive door, but there was nothing that looked like a handle.

Hilda heard a revolting snoring sound from the other side of the door, and something else as well: the patter of tiny hooves.

"Twig," she whispered. "Is that you?"

A quiet whine answered her.

Hilda looked again at the door. The lashes that bound the logs together were made of thick twine. Maybe she could use the torch to burn through the twine and send the logs crashing down on the other side of the entrance.

Too risky, she thought. I might hurt Twig, or wake the sleeping troll.

Perhaps there was another way into the chamber. Hilda retraced her steps and took the narrow path instead. She heard the sound of rushing water and the path led out onto a narrow ledge, high up in the waterfall cavern.

Hilda inched her way along the ledge, feeling the spray on her face, hardly daring to look down at the plunge pool far below.

The ledge became a steep, slippery incline. Hilda threw down the torch and used both hands to haul herself up. She knew that one false move could send her plummeting over the edge and down onto the rocks, but she was an experienced climber, able to find hand and footholds where others could not. As she inched her way up the slope, the sound of snoring confirmed to her that she was on the right track, but then to her surprise and disappointment, the slope leveled out and ended in a vertical wall of rock.

"I don't believe it," muttered Hilda. "Another dead end."

A loud crash came from the chamber above, followed by a high-pitched scream.

"MOM!" cried Hilda.

Looking up at the ceiling, Hilda saw a huge trapdoor with a metal padlock. She bashed it with her fist once, twice, three times, but the lock held fast.

Hilda cast around for something to pick the lock, but all she could see was a rock-chewing slug inching its slimy way across the wall in front of her.

"Hello there," she said, picking it up. "I wonder if you fancy a different sort of snack?"

13

Hilda guessed from Mom's scream that she was having a difficult night, but she had no idea just how difficult. At that exact moment, Mom was teetering on top of a crate, which was balanced on another crate, which in turn was balanced on a tall bookshelf.

Mom's fingers strained upward, toward an opening in the ceiling of the cave. Her way in had been blocked when the troll had heaved the door into place, but if she could only reach up a little bit further, this second opening could prove the perfect escape route for her and Twig.

The bookshelf and the crates were not the most stable ladder Mom could have wished for, and the snoring of the two-headed troll directly below her was a constant reminder of the cost of failure. She had already knocked a shelf off the wall, sending a whole heap of junk cascading down onto the sleeping troll. Why neither head had woken up was still a mystery.

With one final effort, Mom succeeded in hooking her fingertips over the lip of the hole high up in the wall. "Twig!" she called softly. "You go first and I'll follow after! Twig, where are you? Twig! Come here!"

The troll's chamber was a hoarder's paradise, with vast amounts of stuff piled high in every corner. Chairs, baskets, copper pipes, roof tiles, all sorts of junk had found its way into this small cave. And as bad luck would have it, Twig had suddenly become distracted by the discovery of a tiny bird in a cage.

Mom watched helplessly as Twig approached the cage and sniffed at the bird.

TWEET! TWEET! TWEET!

The two-headed troll had remained asleep when a heavy wooden shelf had fallen on its heads, but somehow the twitterings of a tiny bird were enough to wake it up. One eye opened, then two, then three and four, and the first thing those eyes saw was a female human teetering on the top of a makeshift ladder.

A surge of incandescent rage lit up the pair of tiny brains and from the pair of mouths came a bellow so loud that every living creature on the mountainside jumped in fright.

The troll jumped up and reached for Mom. She closed her eyes and winced and—

WHUMP!

A trap door opened in the floor and the troll disappeared through the gap, along with an avalanche of junk. Craning her neck, Mom saw the astonished expression on the troll's two heads as it slid down a rocky slope and over the edge of a precipice.

There was a pause, then Hilda popped her head up through the trap door. "Who would have thought it?" she said. "Rock-eating slugs eat metal, too!"

"Hilda!" Mom scrambled down the makeshift ladder and flung herself into Hilda's outstretched arms. "It's so good to see you!"

"Sorry I didn't stay put," said Hilda, her voice muffled in the front of Mom's sweater.

"I'll let you off, just this once," said Mom.

Twig wriggled up between them, yapping and snuffling, overjoyed at this unexpected reunion.

"Come on," said Mom. "Let's get out of here."

Slowly and carefully, they inched their way down the rocky slope and along the dizzying precipice in the waterfall cavern. Peeking over the edge, Hilda saw the two-headed troll sitting waist deep in the plunge-pool below, alive but dazed.

The troll looked up as they passed, and the sight of the intruders on the ledge above seemed to jog its memory. A furious bellow echoed around the cavern.

"It's wading out of the plunge pool," said Hilda. "It's shaking its fist at us. It's coming this way."

"Enough of the running commentary!" said Mom.

Up the narrow tunnel they ran, then left, then straight, then left again. But it all looked different without a flashlight, and Hilda was far from certain that they were going the right way. The tunnel seemed wider than before, with caves leading off on either side.

"I don't remember this bit!" panted Hilda. "I think we might have taken a wrong—oof!" she tripped over something soft and sprawled on the floor of the tunnel.

"Babababababa," said the soft thing.

"Oh no," said Hilda.

Warm orange light spilled out of a nearby cave.
A shadow passed across the entrance and there
in front of them loomed the mother troll who had
chased them earlier that night.

Heavy footsteps echoed along the tunnel behind
them, and the roaring of the two-headed troll came
closer. The mother troll's eyes widened in fear
and in one quick, decisive movement, she scooped
up Mom, Hilda, and Twig, carried them into
her cave and rolled an enormous boulder across
the entrance. A moment later, the two-headed
troll charged past, its furious footsteps receding
into the distance.

"Babababa!" said the troll child, pointing
at Hilda.

The mother troll's cave was neat and homely,
lit by flickering lamps around the walls. It was
divided into two parts: a kitchen area with shelves
and a cauldron, and a sleeping area around a
cozy-looking fire.

The hour that followed was one of the most extraordinary hours of Hilda's life. The mother troll looked after Hilda and Mom like honored guests. She gave them a blanket and a pillow in the warmest, coziest corner of the sleeping area and brought them each a mug of something warm and sweet that tasted of elderflowers and honey.

As for the troll child, it kept toddling over to Hilda to bring her random gifts: first a carrot, then a sprig of heather, then two small, stone figures. Hilda could not help noticing that one of the figures looked a bit like the troll child, and the other looked like her, with a scarf of leaves and blue yarn for hair.

"So cute," said Hilda sleepily.

Mom spread the blanket over Hilda, then cuddled up with Twig.

The last thing Hilda saw was four glowing of eyes on the far side of the cave: mother and child, watching her intently as she drifted off to sleep...

14

The sun rose over the Great Forest. A flock of pink-footed geese flew over the mountains and crickets whirred and clicked in the grass below.

David wrinkled his forehead and snuggled his head deeper into his pillow, but the pillow was no longer as soft as it had seemed before. It felt strangely rough against his cheek, then crusty and then as hard as stone.

When David opened his eyes, he found that he was sitting upright with one arm around a boulder and his face pressed against it. An empty packet of

Jorts on top of the boulder twitched in the morning breeze, then fluttered to the ground.

"Gah!" cried David, letting go of the troll rock and checking himself to see whether any of his limbs had been bitten off. So far as he could tell, he was intact.

Frida was already awake, watching him with an amused expression.

"Morning," said David, sheepishly. "Do you think it hurts, turning into stone like that?"

Frida shrugged. "I imagine it would make me pretty grumpy."

A loud buzzing came from the Thermos flask at David's feet. The buzzing woke up Gerda, who opened her eyes and smiled sleepily.

"Morning, campers," said Gerda. "You ready to build that blimp?"

"Definitely," said David. "But before we do, we should probably boost our energy with another bag of those excellent Jorts—"

Gerda reached for the emergency rations, then suddenly looked up at the sky. "Watch out!" she yelled, pointing. "It's some kind of crazy pigeon!

It's dive-bombing us!"

"That's not a crazy pigeon," said Frida. "That's Cedric, and the elf on his back is called Alfur. You can't see him unless you sign the paperwork. Morning, Alfur!"

Cedric landed on the troll rock's nose and Alfur dismounted with a flourish. "Tontu came home," he said excitedly. "It took him a while, but he made it back to the apartment safe and sound, and he saw where Hilda and Mom exited limbo."

"Where?" cried Frida and David at the same time. "Where are they?"

"They're closer than you think." Alfur waved
a page from one of Hilda's old sketchbooks, a
map of the valley and the surrounding mountains.
"You see this mountain in the middle of the map,
right here?"

"Boot Mountain?"

"Well, yes," said Alfur, "but that's just Hilda's
silly name for it. We elves call it something much
more fitting."

"What's that?"

"Troll Mountain," said Alfur, lowering his voice
to a sinister whisper. "Tontu is ninety-nine per cent
certain that Hilda and Mom are somewhere inside
Troll Mountain."

Hilda was in the middle of a beautiful dream when she was startled by a troll child jumping on her chest.

"Ba...ba...babababababa," it said.

Hilda tickled the toddler under its chin. "Oof," she said. "You're heavy."

The two mothers were already awake. The troll mother was dragging her finger in the dirt, making a series of strange patterns.

"Morning, Hilda!" said Mom. "Our host is drawing us a map to show us the way out!"

"What's that thing there?" giggled Hilda, pointing to a circle with a squiggly tail drawn in the dirt.

As if in reply, the troll mother closed her fist and lifted it high in the air. When she opened her hand, a snow-white woff was sitting on her palm.

"Whoa!" said Hilda. "How did you do that?"

The troll mother blew gently on the woff, which lit up like a fiery ember and flew away.

"A glow-in the dark woff!" squealed Hilda. "That must be our guide. It's going to lead us out of here!"

"Come on!" cried Mom. "We mustn't lose it!"

The mother troll rolled the boulder away from the cave entrance and the fiery woff flew out into the dark tunnel beyond. Hilda and Mom ran after it, their hearts alive with hope, Twig bounding at their heels.

Hilda paused in the tunnel and looked back. The troll child stood at the entrance to its cave, watching them with big, bright eyes.

"Bye-bye," said Hilda, waving to it. "Thank you both so much!"

The woff guided them through a maze of boulders and tunnels. Mom and Hilda followed at a trot.

"You're loving this, aren't you?" said Mom, smiling down at Hilda.

"Not really," said Hilda. "It's quite nice to be in peril when I know you're waiting for me at home with a nice pie or a freshly baked cake. But it's kind of unnerving when you're actually, you know, here!"

Mom chuckled.

"And no offense," Hilda added, "but you run like a troll."

"I don't run like a troll!"

"Yes, you do," Hilda giggled. "Heavy footed, like a great big troll."

"I don't!"

"Listen to yourself and you'll see what I mean," said Hilda. "Clomp, clomp, clomp!"

"I thought that sound was you!" squealed Mom, laughing so hard she could hardly run straight. "You and your great big boots. Clomp, clomp, clomp."

Hilda frowned. She knew it wasn't her that was clomping, but she certainly wasn't imagining it. If anything, the sound was getting louder.

CLOMP! CLOMP! CLOMP!

A horrible feeling of dread stole over Hilda, and when at last she risked a backward glance, she knew with certainty what she would see.

The two-headed troll was clomping down the tunnel in hot pursuit. Its vicious, bloodshot eyes met Hilda's frightened gaze, and it began to roar its heads off.

"RAAARRRR!!!"

No one was laughing now. Hilda, Mom, and Twig picked up their feet and sprinted down the tunnel as if their lives depended on it, which of course they did.

Even Hilda's speed was no match for this troll. Four enormous fingers and a massive thumb closed around her waist and the next thing she knew, she was no longer running but pedalling her legs in mid-air.

Two slavering mouths yawned open to receive the delicious human morsel, and for a moment it seemed undecided on which of its mouths to feed.

That one second of indecision was what saved Hilda. That, and her plucky deer fox friend, who scrambled up the troll's left leg, then sailed through the air and sank his teeth into its thumb.

"AAAIEEEEE!" roared the troll.

It opened its hand to shake Twig off, allowing Hilda to wriggle out of its grip.

"Well done, Twig!" yelled Mom.

Twig and Hilda hit the ground at the same moment. Mom helped her daughter up and off they shot, sprinting after the fiery woff. They were nearing the end of the tunnel, but the troll was catching up again. Any second now and it would be upon them.

"Coo-roo-catoo!"

A pigeon swooped into the tunnel, ridden by a pointy-hatted elf. As the troll reached out to grab its prey, Cedric flew right in front of its eyes, flapping its wings and cooing its head off.

The troll stumbled and almost fell. It snarled and beat the air in an attempt to swat the pesky pigeon, but Alfur was a skilful rider and he managed to avoid each swipe.

Out of the mountain dashed Hilda, Mom, and Twig, and the distracted troll blundered after them, realizing far too late that a bright new day had dawned.

As soon as the sun's rays hit the troll, the cells of its body began to mutate. Its muscles cooled. Its tendons hardened. Silicon and quartz filled every pore and all four livid eyes sank into flint. As stony and immobile as a statue, the bicephalous troll tumbled heads over heels down the mountainside, a snarl of anguish frozen on each face.

From Alfur's vantage point on pigeonback, it soon became clear that even in its lumpen form the troll was still a threat. The colossal boulder gathered speed as it crashed and bounced through bushes and trees.

"Run faster!" panted Mom as she careered down the hill, pumping her arms like an elite sprinter.

"I'm going as fast as I can!" called Hilda, her yellow scarf streaming out behind her in the wind.

"Implement CAMs!" yelled Alfur suddenly.

Hilda looked up and saw the little elf gesturing at her frantically. "How can I?" she shouted back. "I don't even know what that means!"

"CAMs!" screamed Alfur. "Cliff Avoidance Manoeuvres! There's a steep drop straight ahead of you!"

Hilda realized that they had exited the mountain on the opposite side from where they had gone in. This side of the mountain was not the gently sloping front of the Boot, but the steep and deadly heel. The problem was, she was already running so fast, she was practically in freefall. She could not slow down now even if she wanted to.

Mom was first to reach the precipice. She barrelled off the edge and flew out into nothingness, her arms and legs wheeling helplessly.

"Grab on!" cried a child's voice.

A weighted rope dropped right in front of

Mom. She made a grab for it, held on and let it take her weight, whisking her up and away into the bracing wind.

"Good catch, Hilda's Mom!" cried Frida. "Welcome aboard this BA flight."

"Blimp Air," chuckled David. "Hold tight while we pull you up."

Hilda was thrilled to see her mom was safe, but she knew there was no way the blimp could double back in time to save her, too. Twig was hanging off her pant leg, trying desperately to slow her down, but there was nothing either of them could do.

They dived off the edge of the cliff and fell through the void, faster and faster, cold air whistling past them. Hilda felt a pang of déjà vu as her hat flew off, her sweater billowed, and the ground rushed up to meet her.

15

Mom hugged her rescue rope and stared in horror as Hilda and Twig flew off the edge of the cliff and plummeted toward the ground, followed a moment later by the two-headed troll rock. The rock was so gigantic, it completely hid Hilda and Twig from her view.

"Don't worry!" shouted Frida. "Hilda is a good rider. She's done it loads of times."

"Rider? What do you mean? Done what loads of times?"

A snow-white woff shot up into the air, with

Hilda and Twig on its back. Joyfully it looped the loop and barrel rolled and span.

"I'm on top of the WORLD!" yelled Hilda, laughing.

"Just make sure you hold on tight!" yelled Mom. "And tell that big fluff-ball to stop showing off!"

Hilda buried her face in the soft white fur between the woff's teddy-like ears. "Thank you for saving my life," she whispered. "You're the best rescue vehicle I've ever ridden."

Tears of relief streamed down Mom's cheeks as the magical woff, the emergency blimp, and the goggle-eyed pigeon broke free of Troll Mountain and headed back to Trolberg.

An hour later, Hilda, Frida, David, Gerda, Alfur, and Tontu were seated around the table in Hilda's apartment. Twig dozed contentedly on the sofa and Cedric strutted on a windowsill.

"Hot chocolate for the adventurers," said Mom, coming into the room with a steaming pan. "Shall I pour it into that Thermos flask?

"No!" cried Frida, horrified.

"Ahlbug's in there," said David. "I mean, Erik Ahlberg."

"Is he, really?" Mom laughed. "And Miss Hallgrim is in my snowglobe, I presume."

While Mom went to fetch some mugs, Hilda picked up the Thermos and peered inside. A yellow and brown insect with a Safety Patrol logo on its abdomen looked up at her and buzzed angrily.

"Whoa," said Hilda. "Did you do this, Frida?"

"Not on purpose!" said Frida. "I was trying to do the invisibility spell, but I ended up doing transformation by mistake."

"Do you think you can transform him back?"

"Let me see." Frida took a pinch of castle dust from her pouch and tossed it into the Thermos. She chanted the reverse spell: "Lund Skipta Menskr!"

There was a loud pop and a puff of smoke. When the smoke cleared, Erik Ahlberg was sitting on the table.

"It worked!" cried Frida.

Ahlberg jumped down and rounded on Frida. "How dare you use magic on me?" he snapped. "And as for you, Deputy Gerda, you put me in a Thermos flask!"

"To be fair, sir, you were a bug at the time. It was for your own safety."

"Safety!" Erik Ahlberg tossed his head. "You are fired from the Safety Patrol, Deputy Gerda. And none of you have heard the last of this, I can promise you that!"

Commander Ahlberg tightened his belt, adjusted his cape and hat, and stormed out of the apartment.

Mom returned with a tray of mugs and a big bowl of marshmallows. "Seeing as we are celebrating," she beamed, "I thought we'd have marshmallows in our hot chocolate."

As Hilda slid down between her cool cotton sheets at bedtime, she could not help remembering the rough, woollen blanket she had curled up beneath the previous night. The mother troll had slept without a blanket or pillow, having given her guests everything she owned.

And for what? What had humans ever done for trolls, except drive them from their homeland, build a wall to keep them away and torment them with agonizing, unrelenting bells? By welcoming Hilda and Mom into her home, the mother troll had shown the sort of kindness that people like Erik Ahlberg would never understand.

Mom came in and sat down on the edge of Hilda's bed. "Penny for your thoughts," she murmured.

"I was thinking about those trolls," said Hilda sleepily. "The ones who took us in last night."

"They saved our lives," said Mom. "And I do wish we had the recipe for that honey drink they gave us. That was amazing."

Hilda smiled and nodded. A tear formed in the corner of her eye.

"Hilda, what's wrong?" asked Mom, stroking her hair.

Hilda was determined not to cry. She bit her lip, screwed up her face and tried to think of happy things, but it was no good. "I keep thinking about that moment when you ran back into the mountain to save Twig," she sobbed. "I thought I might never see you again."

Mom leaned down to whisper in her ear. "I'm not going anywhere, Hilda. I love you far too much."

"I know you do. But I've been so horrible to you—" Hilda's words came in short, teary bursts. "Lying and sneaking out and not playing that new Dungeon Crops game even though you've been asking me for weeks—I'm so sorry, Mom! I'll be better, I promise."

"Shush, now." Mom put a finger over Hilda's lips. "You don't need to be better, Hilda. Just don't hide things from me, okay? I'm glad you're the way you are. I'm proud of you. But if you don't tell me what's going on, how do I know you're safe? That's kind of worrying for a mom."

Hilda wiped her eyes on her woff toy. "You really don't wish I was different?"

"I wouldn't change you for the world."

Hilda sat up in bed and they hugged for a long time. Then she lay down again and let Mom tuck

her up tight. As Mom walked away, Hilda felt
Twig jump onto the bed and curl up on her feet.

"No sneaking out, all right?" said Mom,
switching off the light.

"Don't worry about that." Hilda closed her eyes
and snuggled into the pillow. "I'm not getting out
of bed for a week."

How much can you remember from
Hilda and the White Woff? Answer these
fiendish quiz questions to find out!

1. What boardgame does Mom want to play?

2. What kind of plant is big enough to hide a bike in?

3. Name one of the types of food that Hilda, Frida, and David eat in the Great Forest.

4. What kind of bird did Twig save Hilda from?

5. What is Torgund also known as?

6. What is the magic necklace that banishes fear called?

7. What flavor is the pie Mom bakes?

8. Name two members of the Trolberg Safety Patrol.

9. What was David's first Sparrow Scout badge?

10. What kind of animal carries the troll mother's food and bundles?

Answers: 1. Dungeon Crops 2. The giant rafflewort 3. Veggie sausages, crusty baguettes, ginger biscuits, rowanberries 4. A razorback eagle. 5. The Warrior of Thunder 6. The Medallion of Sigurd 7. Spinach and rowanberry 8. Gerda Gustav and Erik Ahlberg 9. First Aid 10. A goat.

WELCOME TO THE PACK!

Do you have what it takes to be a brave and brilliant Sparrow Scout? Learn how in this official guide—with a little help from Hilda. Earn badges, from practical skills like tying knots to the best way to ride a woff.

This illustrated guide contains essential information on magical creatures, from trolls to tide mice. It will even help you to become a nature explorer, just like Hilda! As well as learning about the stars and how to build a shelter, you'll discover loads of tips and tricks on Trolberg life from your favorite blue-haired adventurer.

CYCLING AND HORSEBACK RIDING BADGES

A noble steed is necessary for Sparrow Scouts who want
to get out and about in Trolberg—be it on horseback or by
bicycle. But whether your steed has two wheels or four hooves,
learning how to ride it swiftly and safely is essential!

WOFF RIDING BADGE

Why would anyone bother riding a boring bike or horse when they
could be soaring the skies on the back of a majestic woff? These flying
fluffballs are a brilliant way to get around if you're brave enough to
hop on. Certain to get you to where you want to be (if where you want
to be is wherever they were heading in the first place) this is a top
method of travel for any aspiring adventurer.

OTHER TOP TRANSPORTERS

WEATHER SPIRITS: Super-comfy
cloud seats, but don't listen when you
tell them you want to get off.

THUNDERBIRDS: Very fast and
friendly, but difficult to hold on to.

OLD GIANTS: Excellent views and
good conversation, hard to get
their attention. Oh! And they
smushed our house (to be fair,
it was by accident).

+BADGE POINTS+

To get this badge,
Sparrow Scouts must:

* Bravely jump on a woff
as it whooshes past
(50 points)

* Stay on the woff for
more than four seconds
(100 points)

* Dismount the woff
without breaking any
bones (5,000 points)

HOW TO RIDE A WOFF

1. Wait until the woff has swooped low to the ground, then jog along beside it until you are running at the same speed. Curl your fingers firmly in its fur and JUMP!

2. Woffs get a bit annoyed when somebody tries to ride them, so cling on tightly to its ears. These make excellent handles.

3. If your woff starts jerking and jolting, reassure them that you're just hitching a lift and will jump off soon.

Woffs I have known

4. Don't try to steer. Just enjoy the ride.

5. When the woff swoops low again, leap off and hit the ground running. Hopefully you're happy with where you ended up.

She's a fearless blue-haired girl who travels from her home in a vast magical wilderness, full of elves and giants, to the bustling city of Trolberg. There she meets new friends and mysterious creatures who are stranger —and more dangerous—than she ever expected.

Season 1 now streaming on Netflix.
Season 2 coming in 2020.

PRAISE FOR THE HILDA COMICS

"Pearson has found a lovely new way to dramatise childhood demons, while also making you long for your own cruise down the fjords."
The New Yorker

"Plain smart and moving. John Stanley's Little Lulu meets Miyazaki."
Oscar award-winning Director Guillermo Del Toro

"Hilda is a curious, intelligent, and adventure-seeking protagonist."
School Library Journal

"The art is as whimsical as the protagonist, and the bright colors enhance this comic book's magical realistic effect."
The Horn Book Review

" Luke Pearson's Hildafolk series mixes humor, mystery and fantasy into a superb piece of escapism for young and old alike."
Broken Frontier

PRAISE FOR THE HILDA FICTION

"A fun and pacey adventure combining a contemporary heroine with a gentle mythological element."
BookTrust

"Want to take the kids on a great adventure? Hilda is the one!"
The Great British Bookworm

"I have loved Hilda since the Hildafolk graphic novels, and now the full-length novels are just as good (maybe better)!"
Mango Bubbles

"Dynamic cartoon art brings the book to life, Hilda's bravery is an inspiration, and the world's details—the giant she chats with, the rabbit-riding elf army—will pull readers in."
Publishers Weekly

"The Hilda books are already beloved favorites of many kids; the Netflix series and these chapter books are likely to get her even more fans."
The Beat

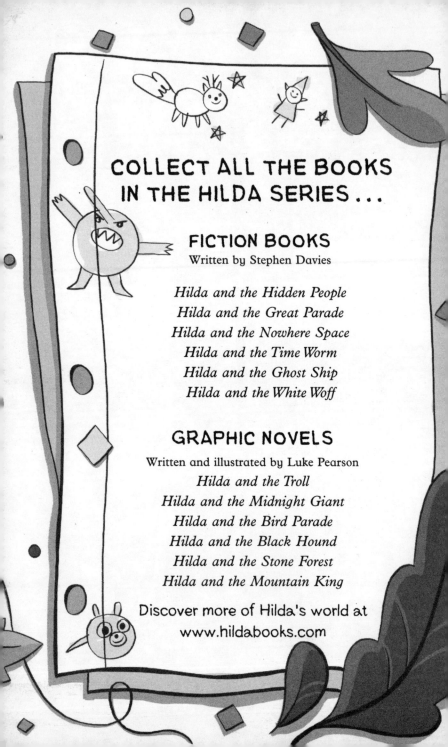

COLLECT ALL THE BOOKS IN THE HILDA SERIES...

FICTION BOOKS
Written by Stephen Davies

Hilda and the Hidden People
Hilda and the Great Parade
Hilda and the Nowhere Space
Hilda and the Time Worm
Hilda and the Ghost Ship
Hilda and the White Woff

GRAPHIC NOVELS

Written and illustrated by Luke Pearson
Hilda and the Troll
Hilda and the Midnight Giant
Hilda and the Bird Parade
Hilda and the Black Hound
Hilda and the Stone Forest
Hilda and the Mountain King

Discover more of Hilda's world at
www.hildabooks.com